Weekly Reader Children's Book Club presents

Giants, Indeed!

Written & illustrated by VIRGINIA KAHL

CHARLES SCRIBNER'S SONS   NEW YORK

Printed in the United States of America/1 3 5 7 9 11 13 15 17 19 RD/C 20 18 16 14 12 10 8 6 4 2
Library of Congress Catalog Card Number 73-14401/ISBN 0-684-13659-7
Weekly Reader Children's Book Club Edition

Once upon a time, long long ago, in a land where fearsome beasts wandered the misty forests and strange creatures swam in the seas, there lived a boy named Christopher.

He lived with his mother and father and sisters and brother in a small cottage at the edge of a village near a winding road that led to the forests.

And he longed to see the rest of the world.

One day, when he felt brave and strong and adventurous, he decided it was time to go see what lay beyond the forests.

"Don't go!" said his father. "There are monsters in the forest, and monsters are dangerous to meet."
Christopher snorted.
"Monsters, indeed!" he said.

"Don't go!" cried his sisters and brother. "There are huge, strange creatures in the seas. If you go near the water, they will snatch you and carry you deep into the sea."
Christopher laughed.
"Strange sea creatures, indeed!" he said.

"Don't go!" wailed his mother. "Worst of all, there are giants roaming the land. They are enormous and fierce, and they eat folk like us. More than anything else, they like little boys."

Christopher laughed. "Giants," he said. "Giants, indeed!"

He paid no attention to the warnings he received. Though his father forbade him to go, though his sisters and brother warned him, though his mother burst into tears, he packed some bread and cheese, put on his stoutest boots, and waved good-bye.

Off he trudged down the long, winding road that led from the village.

By noon Christopher had reached the forest, where giant pines towered over him and where only a little sunlight filtered down onto the path.

He was tired and hungry, so he sat down under a tall tree and leaned against a great green moss-covered boulder. He opened his pack and took out the bread and cheese.

Just as he bit into the crusty brown loaf, he heard a sound behind him. First, there was a wheezy, drawn-out breath; then there was a great rumble; and finally, the great green moss-covered stone he was leaning against stirred and grumbled and groaned.

The great green boulder was no boulder at all!

Christopher jumped to his feet.
Standing high above him, with teeth gleaming, tongue darting back and forth, and jaws gnashing, was the most enormous beast he had ever seen!

"It's a monster!" Christopher cried. "A monster, indeed!"

And before the creature could snatch him in its fearful jaws, Christopher fled.

He forgot his bread; he forgot his cheese; and he forgot that he was getting tired. He just ran and ran and ran, on and on through the dark forest, until the trees grew sparse and the sky grew brighter and he reached the edge of a seemingly endless sea.

He threw himself down at the edge of the sea and tried to catch his breath. By and by he grew calm.

"So there are monsters," he said. "My father was right." As he sat and marveled at his narrow escape, he grew hungrier and hungrier.

"Perhaps I can catch a little fish to eat. There should be something tasty swimming here in the cold, pure water."

He fashioned a hook from a briar, and he tied a vine to it. Then he sat down at the edge of the sea to wait for a fish to bite.

Just as he was beginning to doze in the warm sunshine there was a tremendous jerk on the line, and Christopher flew into the water.

When Christopher was able to shake the water from his eyes, he stared in surprise.

Right beside him was a huge strange creature, puffing and blowing and thrashing its terrible tail.

Its jaws were wide and its teeth were sharp.

Its beady eyes were on him. With a great lunge it reached out for him.

But Christopher plunged away just in time.

Christopher swam to the shore and he ran and ran, away from the endless sea. He forgot that he was hungry; he forgot that he was tired. As fast as he could go, he ran toward the hills that he could see in the distance.

"My sisters and brother were right," thought Christopher as he ran. "There really are strange creatures in the sea."

By the time he reached the hills, the sun had set completely, and a few stars appeared in the sky. Christopher could see nothing but deep, dark shadows. He fell down, exhausted, in a little hollow on the hillside.

As he settled down to sleep where he had fallen, he heard a noise. It was a rustling sound, like that of a great animal.

"Who's there?" he asked in a quavering voice.

There was a long silence; then came a booming voice.

"Who are you?" asked the voice.

"My name is Christopher. Who are you?" the boy asked again, straining to see the speaker.

"Why," answered the voice, "my family and I are travelers. Night overtook us as we were crossing this flat plain, so we are resting here, waiting for the morning light."

Though he could not see the speaker, Christopher was relieved. He let out a long sigh.

"Thank goodness!" Christopher exclaimed. "I've had enough adventures for one day."

"What kind of adventures?" asked his unseen companion curiously.

"Well, I ran away from home. I laughed when my father warned me of monsters. And then I saw one!

"I sneered when my sisters and brother warned me of huge sea creatures. Then I encountered one!

"And I scoffed when my mother warned me of giants. Now I'm afraid I may meet one."

"Ho, ho," said the traveler. "Giants, indeed! We've traveled far, and though we have seen

monsters and strange sea creatures, we have never met a giant. Tell me, how would we know one?"

"Oh," said Christopher, "you'd know. A giant is the biggest creature you'd ever meet—far, far bigger than we are."

"Is that so?" said the traveler. "Why, in all our travels we have never met a creature larger than we are."

"And they are fierce," warned Christopher. "Worst of all, they eat folk like us."

"Well, well," mused the traveler. "We have yet to meet such a fierce creature. Most creatures are fearful and run when we approach. And I'm sure no one would try to eat us."

Christopher began to feel better. Perhaps tomorrow he could travel with this family that had never heard of giants. He closed his eyes and was immediately asleep.

The rest of the night passed quickly. Then the sky lightened and Christopher awoke.

As he looked about, the earth trembled and the hill on which he had slept began to move!

Christopher quickly slid off the hill.

He looked to one side—there was an enormous toe; there was an even more enormous leg; and attached to this was the most enormous body he had ever seen!

He looked to the other side—there was
another enormous pair of legs, another
enormous body; but this one was wearing
a cloak and bonnet. Beyond these, two
more huge bodies were stirring.

Fingers thick as tree trunks uncurled; eyes large as ponds began to open; yawns loud as thunder rent the air.

As Christopher stared, he realized that what he had thought were hills, were in fact four huge bodies lying on the flat plain.

Christopher just had time enough to duck behind the nearest tree before he was seen.

He watched as the family looked around curiously.

"Our friend must have risen early," said one. "To think that he is afraid of giants! Why, there are no such creatures."

And they all chuckled.

"Imagine creatures larger and fiercer than we are," said the largest one. And they all laughed.

"Imagine something that eats folks like us!" exclaimed the wife.

And they howled in delight.

"Speaking of eating," she said, "I thought I caught sight of a little boy running past me just as I woke. He would have made a tasty snack for breakfast."

"Well, I shouldn't worry," said the husband as he pulled on his boots. "There will be others, I'm sure."

Christopher waited no longer. He was off like a shot, streaking along the path he'd come. He ran and ran until he came to the seemingly endless sea. He ran past the sea where the water churned and a huge tail thrashed about.

He ran through the misty forest where the monster was shuffling and wheezing and growling.

He kept running down the long winding road until he was safe in his father's cottage.

His family gathered round to welcome him back, and as he hugged them all at once, he vowed that he'd never leave home again.

As for the family of travelers, they set out on their journey again.

As they trudged on down the road that crossed the flat plain, they shook their heads.

"Giants," they said. "Giants, indeed!"